THE GRUFFALO

Julia Donaldson

Illustrated by Axel Scheffler

MACMILLAN CHILDREN'S BOOKS

Sometimes I feel rather like th~~e~~ I invented the Gruffalo, and no~~w~~ ?een~~s~~ to be ?
bookshops, at birthday parties, in theatres – even once on *The Archers*. I haven't yet
met him in the deep dark wood but that's probably just a matter of time.

The Gruffalo has his tenth birthday this year. Looking back, it's odd to think that he
nearly didn't exist at all. The story was originally going to be about a tiger but I couldn't
find anything to rhyme with that, so I created a monster who rhymed with "know"
(as in, "Silly old Fox, doesn't he know"). Even then, things weren't straightforward.
I nearly gave up writing the story halfway through, because at first I just couldn't find
a neat way of telling the second half in rhyme. "I don't think it's going to be very good
anyway," I told my family. But my son Alastair said, "Don't give up, Mum – I think
it's good!" so I ploughed on.

Of course, the Gruffalo didn't really come to life until Axel had drawn him. I had
vaguely imagined more of an alien-like creature but as soon as I saw Axel's drawing
it was a case of, "Of course, that's what he looks like."

So on this anniversary year, I want to thank both Alastair and Axel. And of course,
I'd like to wish the Gruffalo – along with the mouse, fox, owl and snake –
many happy returns.

Julia Donaldson

For Malcolm and Clémentine
J.D. and A.S.

First published in 1999 by Macmillan Children's Books
This edition published 2009 by Macmillan Children's Books
a division of Macmillan Publishers Limited
20 New Wharf Road, London N1 9RR
Basingstoke and Oxford
Associated companies throughout the world
www.panmacmillan.com

ISBN: 978-0-330-50741-7

Text copyright © Julia Donaldson 1999 and 2009
Illustrations copyright © Axel Scheffler 1999 and 2009
Moral rights asserted.

1 3 5 7 9 8 6 4 2

A CIP catalogue record for this book is available from the British Library.

Printed in Belgium by Proost

A mouse took a stroll through the deep dark wood.
A fox saw the mouse and the mouse looked good.
"Where are you going to, little brown mouse?
Come and have lunch in my underground house."
"It's terribly kind of you, Fox, but no —
I'm going to have lunch with a gruffalo."

"A gruffalo? What's a gruffalo?"
"A gruffalo! Why, didn't you know?

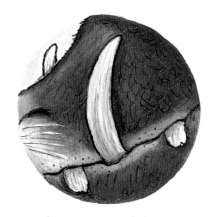

"He has terrible tusks,   and terrible claws,

And terrible teeth in his terrible jaws."

"*Where are you meeting him?*"
"Here, by these rocks,
And his favourite food is roasted fox."

"Roasted fox! I'm off!" Fox said.
"Goodbye, little mouse," and away he sped.

"Silly old Fox! Doesn't he know,
There's no such thing as a gruffalo?"

On went the mouse through the deep dark wood.
An owl saw the mouse and the mouse looked good.
"Where are you going to, little brown mouse?
Come and have tea in my treetop house."
"It's frightfully nice of you, Owl, but no —
I'm going to have tea with a gruffalo."

"A gruffalo? What's a gruffalo?"
"A gruffalo! Why, didn't you know?

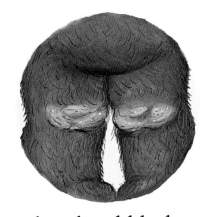

"He has knobbly knees,   and turned-out toes,

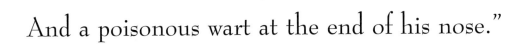

And a poisonous wart at the end of his nose."

"*Where are you meeting him?*"
"Here, by this stream,
And his favourite food is owl ice cream."

"*Owl ice cream? Toowhit toowhoo!*
Goodbye, little mouse," and away Owl flew.

"Silly old Owl! Doesn't he know,
There's no such thing as a gruffalo?"

On went the mouse through the deep dark wood.
A snake saw the mouse and the mouse looked good.
"Where are you going to, little brown mouse?
Come for a feast in my logpile house."
"It's wonderfully good of you, Snake, but no —
I'm having a feast with a gruffalo."

"A gruffalo? What's a gruffalo?"
"A gruffalo! Why, didn't you know?

"His eyes are orange,   his tongue is black;

He has purple prickles all over his back."

"Where are you meeting him?"
"Here, by this lake,
And his favourite food is scrambled snake."

"Scrambled snake! It's time I hid!
Goodbye, little mouse," and away Snake slid.

"Silly old Snake! Doesn't he know,
There's no such thing as a gruffal . . .

. . . Oh!"

But who is this creature with terrible claws
And terrible teeth in his terrible jaws?
He has knobbly knees and turned-out toes
And a poisonous wart at the end of his nose.
His eyes are orange, his tongue is black;
He has purple prickles all over his back.

"Oh help! Oh no!
It's a gruffalo!"

"My favourite food!" the Gruffalo said.
"You'll taste good on a slice of bread!"

"Good?" said the mouse. "Don't call me good!
I'm the scariest creature in this wood.
Just walk behind me and soon you'll see,
Everyone is afraid of me."

"*All right,*" said the Gruffalo, bursting with laughter.
"*You go ahead and I'll follow after.*"

They walked and walked till the Gruffalo said,
"*I hear a hiss in the leaves ahead.*"

"It's Snake," said the mouse. "Why, Snake, hello!"
Snake took one look at the Gruffalo.
"*Oh crumbs!*" he said, "*Goodbye, little mouse,*"
And off he slid to his logpile house.

"You see?" said the mouse. "I told you so."
"*Amazing!*" said the Gruffalo.

They walked some more till the Gruffalo said,
"*I hear a hoot in the trees ahead.*"

"It's Owl," said the mouse. "Why, Owl, hello!"
Owl took one look at the Gruffalo.
"Oh dear!" he said, *"Goodbye, little mouse,"*
And off he flew to his treetop house.

"You see?" said the mouse. "I told you so."
"*Astounding!*" said the Gruffalo.

They walked some more till the Gruffalo said,
"*I can hear feet on the path ahead.*"

"It's Fox," said the mouse. "Why, Fox, hello!"
Fox took one look at the Gruffalo.
"*Oh help!*" he said, "*Goodbye, little mouse,*"
And off he ran to his underground house.

"Well, Gruffalo," said the mouse. "You see?
Everyone is afraid of me!
But now my tummy's beginning to rumble.
My favourite food is — gruffalo crumble!"

"*Gruffalo crumble!*" the Gruffalo said,
And quick as the wind he turned and fled.

All was quiet in the deep dark wood.
The mouse found a nut and the nut was good.

10 years of Gruffalo already! Maybe it's time to let you peek into my sketchbook and see how it all began . . .

After I read the story I started to do some quick little rough drawings in my big sketchbook. "What does a gruffalo look like?" I wondered. I had certainly never seen one, but as he was partly described in the story he wasn't too hard to imagine. I added the horns and a tail and more general monstrosity. I went a bit too far at first. "Too scary for tiny children," said the strict editor. I also thought all the animals would be wearing clothes, as they often do in picture books. But Julia had different ideas and, to be honest, I was relieved . . . how would I have dressed the snake?

After I had sketched out the pictures for the book and my drawings were approved, I went and did the artwork. It was rather hard, and I used up all my greens and browns!

There are many people involved in making a picture book and getting it to its readers. I would like to thank everybody who was involved in the making of *The Gruffalo*, especially Kate, the publisher, and above all Julia for creating the monster in words and writing the story.

Axel Scheffler